ROALD DAHL

The Enormous Crocodile

Illustrated by Quentin Blake

PUFFIN BOOKS

To Sophie—R.D.

PUFFIN BOOKS
Published by the Penguin Group
Penguin Putnam Books for Young Readers,
345 Hudson Street, New York, New York 10014, U.S.A.
Penguin Books Canada Ltd, 10 Alcorn Avenue, Toronto, Ontario, Canada M4V 3B2

First published by Jonathan Cape Ltd, 1978
First published in the United States of America by Alfred A. Knopf, Inc., 1978
Published by Puffin Books, 1993
This edition published by Puffin Books,
a division of Penguin Putnam Books for Young Readers, 2003

1 3 5 7 9 10 8 6 4 2

Text copyright © Roald Dahl, 1978
Illustrations copyright © Quentin Blake, 1978, 2001

THE LIBRARY OF CONGRESS HAS CATALOGED THE PREVIOUS PUFFIN EDITION AS FOLLOWS:
Dahl, Roald.
The enormous crocodile / Roald Dahl; pictures by Quentin Blake.
p. cm.
Summary: The enormous crocodile devises secret plans and a few clever tricks to secure his lunch
only to have them foiled by his neighbors.
ISBN: 0-14-036556-7
[1. Crocodiles—Fiction.] 2. Blake, Quentin, ill. II. Title.
[PZ7.D1515En 1993] [E]—dc20 92-44493 CIP AC

Puffin Books ISBN 0-14-230245-7

Manufactured in China

In the biggest brownest muddiest river in Africa, two crocodiles lay with their heads just above the water. One of the crocodiles was enormous. The other was not so big.

"Do you know what I would like for my lunch today?" the Enormous Crocodile asked.

"No," the Notsobig One said. "What?"

The Enormous Crocodile grinned, showing hundreds of sharp white teeth. "For my lunch today," he said, "I would like a nice juicy little child."

"I never eat children," the Notsobig One said. "Only fish."

"Ho, ho, ho!" cried the Enormous Crocodile. "I'll bet if you saw a fat juicy little child paddling in the water over there at this very moment, you'd gulp him up in one gollop!"

"No, I wouldn't," the Notsobig One said. "Children are too tough and chewy. They are tough and chewy and nasty and bitter."

"*Tough* and *chewy*!" cried the Enormous Crocodile. "*Nasty* and *bitter*! What awful tommy-rot you talk! They are juicy and yummy!"

"They taste so bitter," the Notsobig One said, "you have to cover them with sugar before you can eat them."

"Children are bigger than fish," said the Enormous Crocodile. "You get bigger helpings."

"You are greedy," the Notsobig One said. "You're the greediest croc in the whole river."

"I'm the bravest croc in the whole river," said the Enormous Crocodile. "I'm the only one who dares to leave the water and go through the jungle to the town to look for little children to eat."

"You've only done that once," snorted the Notsobig One. "And what happened then? They all saw you coming and ran away."

"Ah, but today when I go, they won't see me at all," said the Enormous Crocodile.

"Of course they'll see you," the Notsobig One said. "You're so enormous and ugly, they'll see you from miles away."

The Enormous Crocodile grinned again, and his terrible sharp teeth sparkled like knives in the sun. "Nobody will see me," he said, "because this time I've thought up secret plans and clever tricks."

"*Clever tricks?*" cried the Notsobig One. "You've never done anything clever in your life! You're the stupidest croc on the whole river!"

"I'm the cleverest croc on the whole river," the Enormous Crocodile answered. "For my lunch today I shall feast upon a fat juicy little child while you lie here in the river feeling hungry. Good-bye."

The Enormous Crocodile swam to the side of the river, and crawled out of the water.

A gigantic creature was standing in the slimy oozy mud on the riverbank. It was Humpy-Rumpy the Hippopotamus.

"Hello, hello," said Humpy-Rumpy. "Where on earth are you off to at this time of day?"

"I have secret plans and clever tricks," said the Crocodile.

"Oh dear," said Humpy-Rumpy. "I'll bet you're going to do something horrid."

The Enormous Crocodile grinned at Humpy-Rumpy and said:

> *"I'm going to fill my hungry empty tummy*
> *With something yummy yummy yummy yummy!"*

"What's so yummy?" asked Humpy-Rumpy.

"Try to guess," said the Crocodile. "It's something that walks on two legs."

"You don't mean . . ." said Humpy-Rumpy. "You don't *really* mean you're going to eat a little child?"

"Of course I am," said the Crocodile.

"Oh, you horrid greedy grumptious brute!" cried Humpy-Rumpy. "I hope you get caught and cooked and turned into crocodile soup!"

The Enormous Crocodile laughed out loud at Humpy-Rumpy. Then he waddled off into the jungle.

Inside the jungle, he met Trunky the Elephant. Trunky was nibbling leaves from the top of a tall tree, and he didn't notice the Crocodile at first. So the Crocodile bit him on the leg.

"Ow!" said Trunky in his big deep voice. "Who did that? Oh, it's you, is it, you beastly Crocodile. Why don't you go back to the big brown muddy river where you belong?"

"I have secret plans and clever tricks," said the Crocodile.

"You mean you've got *nasty* plans and *nasty* tricks," said Trunky. "You've never done a nice thing in your life."

The Enormous Crocodile grinned up at Trunky and said:

> *"I'm off to find a yummy child for lunch.*
> *Keep listening and you'll hear the bones go crunch!"*

"Oh, you wicked beastly beast!" cried Trunky. "Oh, you foul and filthy fiend! I hope you get squashed and squished and squizzled and boiled up into crocodile stew!"

The Enormous Crocodile laughed out loud and disappeared into the thick jungle.

A bit further on, he met Muggle-Wump the Monkey. Muggle-Wump was sitting in a tree, eating nuts.

"Hello, Crocky," said Muggle-Wump. "What are you up to now?"

"I have secret plans and clever tricks," said the Crocodile.

"Would you like some nuts?" asked Muggle-Wump.

"I have better things to eat than nuts," sniffed the Crocodile.

"I didn't think there *was* anything better than nuts," said Muggle-Wump.

"Ah-ha," said the Enormous Crocodile,

> *"The sort of things that I'm going to eat*
> *have fingers, toe-nails, arms and legs and feet!"*

Muggle-Wump went pale and began to shake all over. "You aren't really going to gobble up a little child, are you?" he said.

"Of course I am," said the Crocodile. "Clothes and all. They taste better with the clothes on."

"Oh, you horrid hoggish croc!" cried Muggle-Wump. "You slimy creature! I hope the buttons and buckles all stick in your throat and choke you to death!"

The Crocodile grinned up at Muggle-Wump and said, "I eat monkeys, too." And quick as a flash, with one bite of his huge jaws, he bit through the tree that Muggle-Wump was sitting in, and down it came.

But just in time, Muggle-Wump jumped into the next tree and swung away through the branches.

A bit further on, the Enormous Crocodile met the Roly-Poly Bird. The Roly-Poly Bird was building a nest in an orange tree.

"Hello there, Enormous Crocodile!" sang the Roly-Poly Bird. "We don't often see you up here in the jungle."

"Ah," said the Crocodile. "I have secret plans and clever tricks."

"I hope it's not something nasty," sang the Roly-Poly Bird.

"*Nasty!*" cried the Crocodile. "Of course it's not nasty! It's delicious."

> *"It's luscious, it's super,*
> *It's mushious, it's duper,*
> *It's better than rotten old fish.*
> *You mash it and munch it,*
> *You chew it and crunch it!*
> *It's lovely to hear it go squish!"*

"It must be berries," sang the Roly-Poly Bird. "Berries are my favorite food in the world. Is it raspberries, perhaps? Or could it be strawberries?"

The Enormous Crocodile laughed so
much his teeth rattled together
like pennies in a piggy bank.

"Crocodiles don't eat berries," he said.
"We eat little boys and girls. And sometimes
we eat Roly-Poly Birds, as well." Very quickly,
the Crocodile reached up and snapped his jaws at
the Roly-Poly Bird. He just missed the Bird, but he
managed to catch hold of the long beautiful feathers
in its tail. The Roly-Poly Bird gave a shriek of terror
and shot straight up into the air, leaving its tail
feathers behind in the Enormous Crocodile's mouth.

At last, the Enormous Crocodile came out of the other side of the jungle into the sunshine. He could see the town not far away.

"Ho-ho!" he said, talking aloud to himself. "Ha-ha! That walk through the jungle has made me hungrier than ever. One child isn't going to be nearly enough for me today. I won't be full up until I've eaten at least three juicy little children!"

He started to creep forward toward the town.

The Enormous Crocodile crept over to a place where there were a lot of coconut trees.

He knew that children from the town often came here looking for coconuts. The trees were too tall for them to climb, but there were always some coconuts on the ground that had fallen down.

The Enormous Crocodile quickly collected all the coconuts that were lying on the ground. He also gathered together several fallen branches.

"Now for Clever Trick Number One!" he whispered to himself. "It won't be long before I am eating the first part of my lunch!"

He took all the coconut branches and held them between his teeth.

He grasped the coconuts in his front paws. Then he stood straight up in the air, balancing himself on his tail.

He arranged the branches and the coconuts so cleverly that he now looked exactly like a small coconut tree standing among the big coconut trees.

Soon, two children came along. They were brother and sister. The boy was called Toto. His sister was called Mary. They walked around looking for fallen coconuts, but they couldn't find any because the Enormous Crocodile had gathered them all up.

"Oh look!" cried Toto. "That tree over there is much smaller than the others! And it's full of coconuts! I think I could climb that one quite easily if you help me up the first part."

Toto and Mary ran toward what they thought was the small coconut tree.

The Enormous Crocodile peered through the branches, watching them as they came closer and closer. He licked his lips. He began to dribble with excitement.

Suddenly there was a tremendous whooshing noise. It was Humpy-Rumpy the Hippopotamus. He came crashing and snorting out of the jungle. His head was down low and he was galloping at a terrific speed.

"Look out, Toto!" shouted Humpy-Rumpy. "Look out, Mary! That's not a coconut tree! It's the Enormous Crocodile and he wants to eat you up!"

Humpy-Rumpy charged straight at the Enormous Crocodile. He caught him with his giant head and sent him tumbling and skidding over the ground.

"Ow-eeee!" cried the Crocodile. "Help! Stop! Where am I?"

Toto and Mary ran back to the town as fast as they could.

But crocodiles are tough. It is difficult for even a hippopotamus to hurt them.

The Enormous Crocodile picked himself up and crept toward the place where the children's playground was.

"Now for Clever Trick Number Two!" he said to himself. "This one is certain to work!"

There were no children in the playground at that moment. They were all in school.

The Enormous Crocodile found a large piece of wood and placed it in the middle of the playground. Then he lay across the piece of wood and tucked in his feet so that he looked almost exactly like a seesaw.

When school was over, the children all came running into the playground.

"Oh look!" they cried. "We've got a new seesaw!"

They all crowded around, shouting with excitement.

"I'll go first!"

"I'll get on the other end!"

"I want to go first!"

"So do I! So do I!"

Then, a girl who was older than the others said, "It's rather a funny knobbly sort of a seesaw, isn't it? Do you think it'll be safe to sit on?"

"Of course it will!" the others said. "It looks strong as anything!"

The Enormous Crocodile opened one eye just a tiny bit and watched the children who were crowding around him. Soon, he thought, one of them is going to sit on my head, then I will give a jerk and a snap, and after that it will be *yum yum yum*.

At that moment, there was a flash of brown and something jumped into the playground and hopped up onto the top of the swings.

It was Muggle-Wump the Monkey.

"Run!" Muggle-Wump shouted to the children. "All of you, run, run, run! That's not a seesaw! It's the Enormous Crocodile and he wants to eat you up!"

The children screamed and ran for their lives.

Muggle-Wump disappeared back into the jungle, and the Enormous Crocodile was left all alone in the playground.

He cursed the monkey and waddled back into the bushes to hide.

"I'm getting hungrier and hungrier!" he said. "I shall have to eat at least four children now before I am full up!"

The Enormous Crocodile crept around the edge of the town, taking great care not to be seen.

He came to a place where they were getting ready to have a fair. There were slides and swings and dodgem-cars and people selling popcorn and cotton candy. There was also a big merry-go-round.

The merry-go-round had marvelous wooden creatures for the children to ride on. There were white horses and lions and tigers and mermaids with fish tails and fearsome dragons with red tongues sticking out of their mouths.

"Now for Clever Trick Number Three," said the Enormous Crocodile, licking his lips.

When no one was looking, he crept up onto the merry-go-round and put himself between a wooden lion and a fearsome dragon. He sat up a bit on his back legs and he kept very still. He looked exactly like a wooden crocodile on the merry-go-round.

Soon, all sorts of children came flocking into the fair. Several of them ran toward the merry-go-round. They were very excited.

"I'm going to ride on a dragon!" cried one.

"I'm going on a lovely white horse!" cried another.

"I'm going on a lion!" cried a third one.

And one little girl, whose name was Jill, said, "*I'm* going to ride on that funny old wooden crocodile!"

The Enormous Crocodile kept very still, but he could see the little girl coming toward him. "Yummy-yum-yum," he thought. "I'll gulp her up easily in one gollop."

Suddenly there was a *swish* and a *swoosh* and something came swishing and swooshing out of the sky.

It was the Roly-Poly Bird.

He flew round and round the merry-go-round, singing, "Look out, Jill! Look out. Look out. Don't ride on that crocodile!"

Jill stopped and looked up.

"That's not a wooden crocodile!" sang the Roly-Poly Bird. "It's a real one! It's the Enormous Crocodile from the river and he wants to eat you up!"

Jill turned and ran. So did all the other children. Even the man who was working the merry-go-round jumped off it and ran away as fast as he could.

The Enormous Crocodile cursed the Roly-Poly Bird and waddled back into the bushes to hide.

"I'm so hungry now," he said to himself, "I could eat six children before I am full up!"

Just outside the town, there was a pretty little field with trees and bushes all around it. This was called The Picnic Place. There were several wooden tables and long benches, and people were allowed to go there and have a picnic at any time.

The Enormous Crocodile crept over to The Picnic Place. There was no one in sight.

"Now for Clever Trick Number Four!" he whispered to himself.

He picked a lovely bunch of flowers and arranged it on one of the tables.

From the same table, he took away one of the benches and hid it in the bushes.

Then he put himself in the place where the bench had been.

By tucking his head under his chest, and by twisting his tail out of sight, he made himself look very much like a long wooden bench with four legs.

Soon, two boys and two girls came along carrying baskets of food. They were all from one family, and their mother had said they could go out and have a picnic together.

"Which table shall we sit at?" said one.

"Let's take the table with the lovely flowers on it," said another.

The Enormous Crocodile kept as quiet as a mouse. "I shall eat them all," he said to himself. "They will come and sit on my back and I will swizzle my head around quickly, and after that it'll be *squish crunch gollop*."

Suddenly a big deep voice from the jungle shouted, "Stand back, children! Stand back! Stand back!"

The children stopped and stared at the place where the voice was coming from.

Then, with a crashing of branches, Trunky the Elephant came rushing out of the jungle.

"That's not a bench you were going to sit on!" he bellowed. "It's the Enormous Crocodile, and he wants to eat you all up!"

Trunky trotted over to the spot where the Enormous Crocodile was standing, and quick as a flash he wrapped his trunk around the Crocodile's tail and hoisted him up into the air.

"Hey! Let me go!" yelled the Enormous Crocodile, who was now dangling upside down. "Let me go! Let me go!"

"No," Trunky said. "I will not let you go. We've all had quite enough of your clever tricks."

Trunky began to swing the Crocodile round and round in the air. At first he swung him slowly.

Then he swung him faster . . .

And FASTER . . .

And FASTER . . .

And FASTER STILL . . .

Soon the Enormous Crocodile was just a blurry circle going round and round Trunky's head.

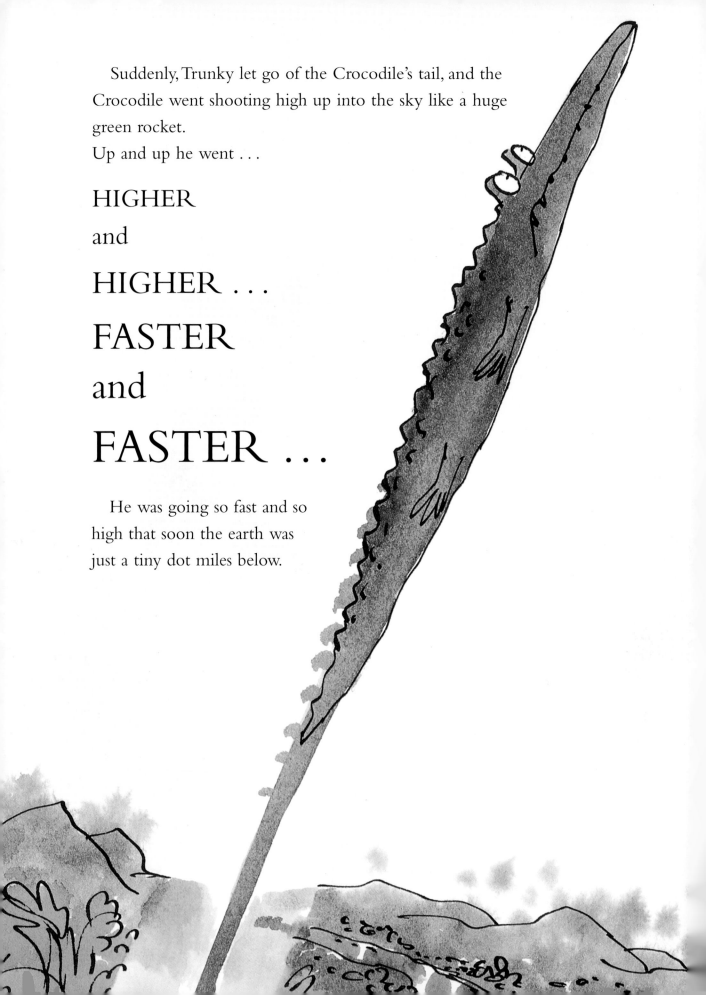

Suddenly, Trunky let go of the Crocodile's tail, and the Crocodile went shooting high up into the sky like a huge green rocket.

Up and up he went . . .

HIGHER

and

HIGHER . . .

FASTER

and

FASTER . . .

He was going so fast and so high that soon the earth was just a tiny dot miles below.

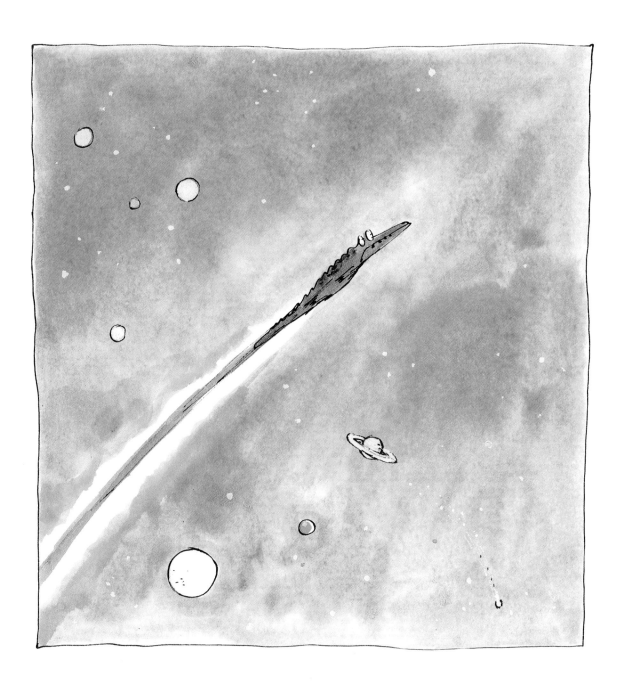

He whizzed on and on.

He whizzed far into space.

He whizzed past the moon.

He whizzed past stars and planets.

Until at last . . .

With the most tremendous

BANG!

the Enormous Crocodile crashed
headfirst into the hot hot sun.

And he was sizzled up like a sausage!